Late Nights at Full Moon Records

A Novella

Sarah Edmonds

Late Nights at Full Moon Records
Copyright © 2023 Sarah Edmonds
All rights reserved.

No part of this publication may be reproduced, distributed, or transmitted in any form or by any means, including photocopying, recording, or other electronic or mechanical methods, without the prior written permission of the publisher, except in brief quotations embodied in critical reviews, citations, and literary journals for noncommercial uses permitted by copyright law.

This is a work of fiction. Names, characters, businesses, places, events, locales, and incidents are either the products of the author's imagination or used in a fictitious manner. Any resemblance to actual persons, living or dead, or actual events is purely coincidental.

ISBN-13: 979-8-9861105-9-2
Cover art and design by Angelo Maneage
Edited by Olivia Zarzycki
Printed in the U.S.A.

For more titles and inquiries, please visit:
www.thirtywestph.com

This book is dedicated to my family and friends who have always supported me, to Rachel for helping me talk through every twist and plot hole, and to anyone who feels lost in their own skin.

May you find the family you need.

Table of Contents

Track 1	1
Track 2	10
Track 3	12
Track 4	20
Track 5	23
Track 6	36
Track 7	43
Track 8	54
Track 9	56
Track 10	60
Track 11	66
Track 12	68
Track 13	72

*"I shall be gone to what I understand,
And happier than I ever was before."*

—Edna St. Vincent Millay,
I shall go back again to the bleak shore

Late Nights at Full Moon Records

Track 1

Full Moon Records stood as part of the main thoroughfare Slatington had to offer—not that that was much. As one of the oldest-running vinyl shops in the county, Full Moon Records was second in town attractions only next to the local drive-in theater. For Lane, the quaint little shop nestled into the ground floor of an old brick townhouse was his last and only option.

Standing outside of the shop, he tried to surreptitiously sniff the collar of his jacket as he put change in the parking meter. He had been sleeping in his car for a month and a half while putting in applications across all the surrounding towns. The jacket was passable—a hand-me-down from when he had attended his great-grandmother's funeral, sometime before his dad's old clothes stopped sitting right on his shoulders. It was too small now to button over his pulp-style t-shirt. His hair was a mess, sticking out in odd angles around his chin, but there wasn't that much he could do about that. Pulling his dismayingly meager resumé out of his back pocket, Lane took a deep breath, put on his best customer service smile, and stepped inside.

"We'll be with you in a minute!" A soft, feminine voice called out from somewhere above him.

"No rush," he replied, leaning over the banister of the large wooden staircase that dominated the right side of the small space. It led to a blue-painted door with its own deadbolt. The owner's apartment.

The shop itself was empty. Lane wandered through the rows of records, organized by release year rather than genre, admiring the art that covered the walls. There were murals of almost every major music period featuring some musicians he recognized—from Bessie Smith to Beyoncé—and many more that he didn't. An old gramophone with a large brass horn stood in the corner facing out across the more contemporary displays of headphones and shop merchandise. He tilted his head to read what was set up to play. *Between the Lines (Remastered)* by Janis Ian.

Lane pulled out his phone and was typing the title into his notes to look up later when the sound of creaking on the staircase drew his attention back to the front. He shoved his phone into his back pocket and met the shop owners by the door.

Two elderly women—Lane guessed they were both in their mid to late 70s—descended the stairs arm-in-arm. One of them, the taller, was in a baby blue dress, the same kind he would have expected his grandmother to wear to church. She seemed to be supporting her shorter counterpart, discretely, while they descended. The shorter woman had salt-and-pepper curls that barely brushed the tops of her ears; she was dressed much more casually, in black slacks, one of the store-branded t-shirts, and a loose red cardigan. Lane felt a slight twinge of concern, wondering how safe it was for the two women to leave their shop open and unattended just steps from the entrance to their home.

"Can we help you?" The woman in the cardigan asked, slightly out of breath, as they reached the bottom of the stairs.

"No, actually," Lane offered his resumé and held out his hand, "I had called about the open position earlier in the week."

"Oh, you must be Elaine!" The taller woman shook his hand while her partner took his resumé.

Lane's smile fell, a light tinge of dread settling in his stomach. "It's just Lane. How did you—"

"You didn't leave a name on your message." The shorter woman raised an eyebrow at him, pointing out his name on his resumé to her companion. "We had to check the Caller ID."

"Right. I forgot about that." Lane felt like there was a never-ending list of things that needed changing. At least if he got a job, he could get a pre-paid phone in his own name. The icy feeling in his stomach spread as the two women shared a knowing glance between themselves. "I'm sorry. If there's any problem—"

"Oh lord no." The woman in the cardigan snorted, clapping him hard on the back. Lane jumped, but her reaction put him a bit more at ease.

"Paperwork is always in the way, isn't it?" The taller woman winked. Her smile looked pained. She turned and her partner and Lane followed her over to the front counter. "Could always use a strong young man around the shop. I'm Dawn and this is my wife, Gayle."

"Nice to meet you." Lane shook Dawn's hand across the counter. She held on a beat longer than necessary and Lane relaxed further.

He had tried not to assume anything about Dawn and Gayle's relationship when he first saw them—in that part of Pennsylvania, making the wrong assumption about the wrong person would lead to being cursed out, at best, and he desperately needed the job—but the knowing air around Dawn when he corrected her about his name made much more sense in context. The couple certainly knew how "in the way" paperwork could be.

Gayle handed his resumé over to Dawn, turning her attention from the paper, her eyes raking over him instead. Lane did his best not to fidget under the shorter woman's gaze. "Cursed?"

"Not that I know of?" Lane answered on reflex, still thrown from the confusion and accidental outing of his phone call.

His cheeks grew hot when Gayle laughed. "Good to know."

"Your shirt, she means," Dawn explained, gesturing to his chest with his resumé. "The movie?"

"Oh!" Lane pulled on the hem of his shirt and looked down to remind himself what he was wearing. Christina Ricci, eyes glowing yellow, stared back up at him through the gap in his jacket's lapels. "Oh right. Yeah. I haven't had the chance to buy anything formal that isn't…"

He trailed off, holding his hands out at his sides as if to pinch the pleats of a skirt. By the expression on Gayle's face, he probably looked more like a penguin.

"We don't have much of a dress code here, so that wouldn't be a problem." Dawn brushed off his excuse, smacking Gayle playfully on the arm to stop her laughing.

Gayle scowled playfully at her wife. "What? It's a great film."

"You're into horror?" Lane couldn't keep the surprise from his voice.

"Old people can't have fun, too?" Gayle crossed her arms but Lane was starting to catch on to the playful quirk of her eyebrow.

"Favorite movie?"

"*Trick 'r Treat.*"

"I like *When Animals Dream*, myself," Dawn chimed in. She had settled onto a stool behind the counter and was watching them from over the top of a pair of rounded reading glasses as she skimmed his resumé. Lane tried not to be overly anxious at the occasional marks she was writing on the paper's margins.

"Do you like *Let the Right One In*, then?" He asked eagerly. If his lack of sales experience had let him down, he could at least win them over with small talk.

"Better than the American one." Dawn shrugged, not truly answering his question. "Do you enjoy vampire films, too, then?"

"I'll watch pretty much anything, but werewolves are highly underrated." Lane shook his head. "There's so much variety. And really, if people want a tortured soul to pity, why not pick the monster that tears itself apart instead of Stoker's mascot for the dangers of homoerotic penetration? I'm all for reclaiming it, though, ya know?"

Lane realized a beat too late how unprofessional his remark had been. Both women just stared at him as he fumbled around for the best way to apologize. It felt downright crass to talk about penetration with women old enough to be his grandmother. Gayle spoke before he had the chance to recover himself.

"Team Jacob, then?"

Lane blinked, having no idea how to reply as both women broke out into laughter. While he stood there, Gayle reached behind her, pulled out a stack of navy-blue t-shirts, and dropped them onto the counter.

"I'm kidding. A lot of our regulars here love to out-indie each other, so we've had to keep up with the pop culture to maintain our reputation." Gayle snorted, then added, "Might want to leave out penetration though."

Her remark earned another swat on the arm from her wife. Lane's ears grew even hotter. Taking off her reading glasses, Dawn looked him over with a more professional eye. "You don't have much retail experience."

"I went to tech school in high school, welding and metallurgy, but my parents wanted me to go to college," Lane explained, not quite as nervous as before. "They didn't let me get a part-time job so that I had time for sports and studying."

"And that didn't work out?"

"They decided they wouldn't pay my tuition if I…" Lane tried, unsuccessfully, to pull his jacket closed at the top button. If only he had something less form-fitting. He cleared his throat and continued, "I didn't have enough saved up and loans didn't pan out because of my parents' money. I never really wanted to go, though, so it's fine. I'm job hunting now so I can save up enough to apply for apprenticeships out of state."

"We're looking for a candidate who's a little more long-term." Dawn frowned.

Lane silently cursed himself. He had tried to make his prospects sound more promising than they were. In reality, he needed money for food—not an out-of-state apartment. He just hadn't wanted them to think he was desperate.

But he was.

Backtracking, he began, "I'm hoping to save up for a while. At least a year or two, but I could—"

"Long-term or not, we need someone now," Gayle interrupted. "It's not like we've got candidates lining the street."

Lane bit his lower lip, silently thanking every horror film he had ever seen that Gayle seemed to be on his side.

"I thought you said we didn't need a part-timer?" Dawn folded her arms, disbelief on her face. "'We don't need some teenager who'll play that yee-haw music all day,' were your exact words, if memory serves."

"Well." Gayle huffed slightly before throwing a question at Lane. "How old are you?"

"Twenty." He may have exaggerated.

"You like country music?"

"No?" The truth, even though it sounded like a question.

"He's perfect!" Gayle clapped him on the back again and he tried not to wince.

"I guess she's decided." Dawn chuckled, slipping her hand through the crook of Gayle's arm. Gayle grinned, taking half a step closer. "Can you come in Monday? We'll sort out the details then, if you're interested."

"Don't you want references?" Lane asked. Not that he had any—unless they counted his high school shop teacher. "I'm not complaining, of course. I mean, thanks?"

Gayle gathered up the pile of shirts from the counter and dropped them into his hands. "I've a way of sniffing out the good ones."

Dawn rolled her eyes and this time Lane chuckled along with them. He had actually done it. They were going to hire him. The relief and gratitude he felt was enough to make him giddy.

"Thank you," Lane repeated once his mind caught up with him. "I'll see you Monday, then?"

"For that damned paperwork." Dawn winked.

The two elderly women saw Lane to the shop door and he tried not to feel too self-conscious when his car backfired as he pulled away from the sidewalk.

Track 2

The hood of Lane's rusted old Taurus vibrated haltingly through the soles of his shoes. He sat on the roof of the car, the light-polluted, grey-blue night sky stretched out above his head, a pile of papers fluttering on his lap. Just above the rustling of dry Autumn grass, music drifted up and out from the open driver's side window. Lane's phone was perched on the edge of the car's roof, his charger barely long enough to string down through the window to the cigarette lighter. He checked the stack of papers against his list twice. Social security card, driver's license, birth certificate, passport. He wasn't exactly sure what all he would need to fill out the hiring paperwork—he had never held a legitimate job before—but he was at least glad his parents had given him enough time to grab everything important before they changed the locks.

Sliding down from the roof of the car, he reached through the window and turned the keys out of the ignition. He had been parking overnight at the edge of some farmer's land on the outskirts of town. Without the sound of traffic or his static-prone car radio, the silence was eerie.

He stashed the documents in the pocket in the back of the driver's seat and pulled a blanket off of the floor.

Though he wasn't much a fan of the bugs, the weather was too nice to sleep in his car again. Instead, he stretched out on top of the blanket and laid on his back, staring up into the sky. The moon was barely there, a crescent no larger than the white curve at the tip of his thumbnail. It provided just enough light for him to see a shadow of the tall grass tickling the hair on his arms.

"Hi, welcome to Full Moon Records. How can I help you today?"

Lane cleared his throat and tried again.

"Hi, welcome to Full Moon Records. Can I help you find anything?"

He frowned, lowering his voice another tone. "Hi, welcome to Full Moon—"

The forced deeper pitch caught a tickle in the back of his throat and set him coughing. He grabbed a half-empty bottle of Mountain Dew by the back tire, chugged what was left, and tossed the bottle back through the open window.

He continued practicing late into the night, the silver crescent rising high into the sky.

Track 3

"Good morning." Dawn met him at the door ten minutes before the store was set to open. "I'm glad to see the shirts fit."

"They do, thanks." Lane's voice was a bit hoarse but not so much that it hurt. More like he had a cold than that he smoked three packs a day. It was passable, at least. "I forgot to ask, is the cost for the shirts taken out per paycheck, or...?"

He didn't have the cash to pay for them out of pocket.

"Oh no, they're yours." Dawn led him back around behind the counter. "We require you to wear them, we can afford to give you them."

"I wish all jobs thought that way."

"I'd like to think we're kinder than most employers." Her tone was more sympathetic than he had expected. Lane felt a twinge of embarrassment, hoping she hadn't been able to tell that he couldn't afford the shirts if she had asked him to pay for them. There was a beat of awkward silence as Dawn opened a drawer in the counter and rifled through a pile of papers. "We'll need your license and social security card, and you'll just need to sign these."

"You must've been looking for someone for a while."

Lane took the offered papers and set about filling them out while Dawn booted up an outdated computer and the equally dusty copier that was plugged into it. "For the position, I mean. That you hired me right away."

"You called about a week after we put the sign up. We've had a few applicants, mostly high schoolers." She stifled a small conspiratorial smile. When she continued, however, her expression turned troubled, the delicate wrinkles around her eyes deepening. Her pink-painted lips puckered. "We've been putting it off for a while now. Prefer to keep to our quiet little corner of town. Gayle, especially, thought a new hire would be more trouble than they're worth. But we're getting older and what with...well, let's just say it's about time we had some help."

"I hope I'll be worth the trouble, then." Lane tried to lighten the mood as he handed the papers back to her. Before he could press the subject further, however, a door from the back of the shop opened, creaking loudly on its hinges.

"You haven't scared him away yet, have you?" Gayle appeared in the doorway with a large box of cleaning supplies in her arms. It was piled so high Lane had trouble seeing her face.

"Let me help you with that." He rushed over and took the box from her hands, surprised by its weight. He had always assumed that elderly people were, for lack of a better word, frail.

"Thanks." She pulled a large metal key from her pocket and locked the door behind her. "Just set it on the counter."

Lane did as she asked, mildly curious about why she felt the need to lock up their cleaning supplies. Dawn cleared room for him to set the box down, returning his license and social security card to him once his hands were free. He avoided her bemused gaze as he glanced down at the date of birth listed on his license. Thankfully, she said nothing as he slipped the documents back into his pocket.

"I thought you opened at nine?" Lane commented, noticing the time on the computer screen had passed the hour mark. The closed sign still hung in the door and neither woman seemed eager to remove it.

"We're keeping the shop closed today," Dawn answered as she clicked the wheezing computer off.

"Deep clean and training day all in one." Gayle joined them at the desk and dropped her key into one of the drawers. "It's your lucky day."

"Just tell me where to start." Lane grabbed a container of antibacterial wipes out of the box and eyed the aisles of records and all the nooks and crannies that dust could hide in. He tried not to look too daunted.

Gayle clapped him on the back and pointed him over to

the glass display cases in the windows. Together, she and Dawn walked him through the different price brackets of the vintage, new, and used-but-modern records that were mixed together across the shop. Dawn looked horrified when he took notes on his phone and Gayle practically shoved a spiral notebook and pen into his hands. The register was, thankfully, straightforward but Lane couldn't hide his alarm at their informal money storage system. The shop wasn't equipped to take anything but cash which meant when collectors came in looking for the rare and unusual, they would sometimes end up with upwards of $300 kept "tucked away" in a Ziplock bag in a wooden jewelry box under the desk—and that didn't even cover the cash they kept on hand for change throughout the day. When Lane suggested a security system, they just cited the low crime rate and their box monitor computer as an excuse against it.

Lane gaped at them. "You should at least get a guard dog or something."

Gayle laughed so hard she had to excuse herself to their apartment above the shop.

"Don't mind her," Dawn laid a hand on his shoulder, rolling her eyes as she watched Gayle ascend the stairs. "And don't worry about us. No one thinks much about a rundown old record shop and a pair of little old ladies."

"But that's exactly why." Lane felt a rock in the pit of his stomach at the thought of the couple sleeping above the shop with little more than a lock to keep them safe. "At least look into an alarm?"

"Sure." Dawn patted his shoulder. "But you'll have to handle setting it up. I hate all those automated techy things."

"Deal."

"Now," Dawn waved for him to go on ahead of her, "let's continue the tour, shall we."

She walked him through the storage closets where they kept the extra boxes of shop merchandise and signage for annual sales, then showed him how to work the vintage gramophone and which records were "store approved" to play during the day. Not a country singer to be found. Lane had only heard of half of the artists in the pile but, when Dawn started the Janis Ian record he had forgotten to look up, he decided he could trust their music taste.

"Upstairs, as you know, is our apartment." Dawn pointed up to the large blue door Gayle had disappeared behind. Lane wondered why she hadn't yet reappeared. "Feel free to knock if you need anything or to join us for lunch, if you like. We don't often keep the door locked."

Lane opened his mouth to point out, again, how unsafe they were being, but Dawn continued on before he could.

"The cleaning supplies are back there," she nodded over to the door from which Gayle had appeared earlier, "but if you need anything just ask one of us and we'll go get it for you. The basement isn't exactly…finished so we'd rather not risk anyone getting hurt."

"What if you're not around?" Lane asked. He could have sworn the stairway had looked pristine when he took the box from Gayle, but he chose not to mention it. "Or if there's an emergency or something?"

"Wait for us to get back." Dawn shook her head. She made sure he met her eyes, her tone sterner than he had yet heard it. "If you only remember one thing from today, don't ever go through that door. Understood?"

Lane nodded, fighting the urge to take half a step back under the severity of her tone. "Yes, ma'am."

"Ma'am." The click of the apartment door shutting drew both of their attention up the stairs. Gayle descended slowly, favoring her right leg, somehow still laughing. "Don't let her fool you, Lane. She's no 'ma'am' any more than I am."

"Unlike you, some people know how to respect their elders." Dawn lifted her chin, indignant, even as she helped Gayle down the remaining steps.

Lane tried to take comfort in their easy banter, but he couldn't shake the sudden apprehension that had swelled in his chest at Dawn's sudden mood change. He tried to shake the feeling. The pair didn't seem very familiar with how to train a new employee—maybe she had been overly severe on accident—and he was, after all, a stranger still. Then again, so were they.

"She tell you about the basement?" Gayle ignored the jab.

"Don't go in no matter what?" Lane tried not to let his uneasiness show.

"Good boy."

The cooing voice Gayle used earned an exasperated sigh from her wife and Lane laughed along with them to cover his confusion. They continued talking him through the last few rules and quirks they had about the way the shop should be run and Lane took notes, as he had been, on everything they said. But he was distracted. It was a simple door, all but disappearing under the paint of the murals that lined the walls. Only really visible as a gap between the shelves of records hugging the perimeter of the room. A simple brass doorknob with its old-fashioned keyhole. A large white, black, and red sign warning customers—and, apparently, him—to keep out.

It was entirely unassuming, but the door stood out in the back of his mind. A nagging question, a curiosity, worrying against his focus as he tried to retain every word of instruction and advice the two women threw his way.

The day ended sooner than he had expected, measured only by the ache in his feet and the glaringly blank spaces on his page of notes.

"We'll be open tomorrow, so come ready for a bustling day," Dawn warned him with enthusiasm, Gayle shaking her head behind her.

Lane held up the borrowed notebook. "I'll be ready."

Track 4

The parking lot outside of the local YMCA was practically empty. Lane shut off his car and grabbed his small duffle out of the backseat, thanking all the residents of Slatington for finding more reasonable hours to exercise. High flickering streetlights marked his path as he jogged across the lot to the glowing glass doors.

"Hello." The secretary greeted him from the front desk. He was a young man, younger than Lane himself, with bright orange hair and thick-lensed glasses. "ID?"

Lane handed over his membership card, avoiding looking at the photograph or name on it. His parents had set up the membership back when they thought he would try to get into college on a softball scholarship. They hadn't let him change his name or the photograph on it, but he was just grateful the card still worked.

Lane nodded, as the secretary checked him into the system, to the security guard whose name he believed was Monica. He had never asked, though, and her perpetual glare kept him from looking at the nametag on her chest long enough to check.

"You're all set." The secretary handed him his ID back with hardly a sideways glance, for which he was grateful.

"Thanks."

Lane kept his head down as he followed the hallway past the equipment room, pool, and sauna. At the end of the hall, he completed a quick survey of his surroundings. The only person to be seen was a woman running on one of the treadmills. Relieved, Lane turned left into the men's locker room.

Lehigh County may have voted blue in the last election, but the abundance of Drain the Swamp flags around town would have anyone thinking otherwise.

The privacy of the facility's individual showers felt divine. Lane turned the water almost as hot as it would go and tilted his face up to the showerhead. The water fell soft over his skin, slowly soaking into his thick brown hair, and sending shivers down his spine. He knew the yearly membership would end in a few months, as would his cell phone service, if his parents didn't renew it—and they had no reason to. With luck, sleeping in his car and living off vending machine food and lunches in the doily-filled apartment with Gayle and Dawn would allow him to save up enough money to find an apartment before then. All of his friends—all three of them—had gone off to college and his pride wouldn't let him ask their parents if he could use their showers, let alone sleep on their couches.

Lane shook himself, reaching blindly for the shampoo

he had brought with him. He would find a way eventually. That was the whole point of applying at the record store, after all. They paid better than any of the other openings in town—at least of the ones he was somewhat qualified for—and, after a week and a half of working with them, Gayle and Dawn seemed like the best employers he could have asked for. So what if they had quirks or a creepy basement?

The warm water and methodical motions slowly relaxed some of the tension from his shoulders. It had been a while since he had felt comfortable in his hometown. Longer than he liked to admit. No matter what happened moving forward, no matter how many nights he had to shower at the gym or sleep in his car or check vending machines for change to spend at the local laundromat, he was grateful to Gayle and Dawn for allowing him that.

Track 5

"Hi, welcome to Full Moon Records, can I help you find anything?"

"I know this store better than you."

Lane gritted his teeth, his smile plastered onto his face as a thin and surprisingly sweaty man passed him and made a beeline for the '80s section of the store.

"Now Michael," Dawn chided the man from where she and Gayle were hanging a Halloween-themed sign in the window, "be nice."

"I don't have any compunction against telling Lane here to charge you double," Gayle added, not bothering to even turn around.

Lane raised an eyebrow as the man, Michael, who was old enough to be his father, turned around sheepishly and shook his hand.

"Sorry man."

Lane shrugged, surreptitiously wiping his hand on his pant leg. "No foul."

Michael hardly waited for his response before returning to the stacks. Gayle cleared her throat, drawing Lane's attention away from him. She jerked her thumb up and winked.

Lane bit back a smile and nodded.

He had been working with Dawn and Gayle for a little more than two weeks when they finally let him in on their secret for dealing with each kind of customer. There were those passing by who stopped in due to the novelty of a record store in such an unpopulated small town; those were treated cordially, with nothing remarkable to note. The regulars, though, could be divided into three categories. The arrogant ones, like Michael, were charged the marked price with tax and—as Gayle's gesture indicated—Lane made sure to move the truly valuable records upstairs, setting them on the coffee table in the apartment sitting room.

It wasn't that Dawn and Gayle were against selling to people like Michael—in fact, Lane soon found, most of the shop's income depended on it—but they liked to say that to sell the classics to someone who would buy records exclusively for the prestige of them went against the very principles the store was founded on. In fact, they often went out of their way to sell those same records at a discounted price to the younger generations, to the middle and high schoolers who stopped in on their way home from school, or who hung around in between class and marching band practice. It wasn't the most fiscally responsible decision, but the two women said that those customers were the ones who would appreciate the music most.

The final type of customer Lane encountered in the shop was the most casual. The people who had their tastes and stuck to them, who could be persuaded with the right nudge to try something new, and who were friendly, generally easy to make small talk with, but never anything deeper. They were his favorite kind of customer.

But he would deal with people like Michael with a smile if it meant he could move out of his car. The heater had started to wear out and Autumn was in full swing.

"Lane, help us with this, will you?" Dawn called over her shoulder as the door chimed shut behind Michael—the man had left without buying anything.

"Sure." Lane set the retrieved box of records back by the specialty display case and joined the couple at the window.

Pulling the rickety step stool over, he climbed up and secured the corner of the sign to the window frame. He leaned over to tie up the other side and felt Dawn's hands on his waist, steadying him.

"Thanks," he said, hopping down directly from the top step.

"No, thank you." Dawn squinted up at the sign with approval. "I hated her climbing up on that thing."

"I'm not too old for a little hard work." Gayle huffed as she put the step stool back in its place.

"We both are, darling, why do you think I kept pushing you to hire someone?"

Gayle grumbled something unintelligible in response. Leaving Lane and Dawn to arrange the oversized plastic pumpkins on top of the window ledge, she went to the door and flipped the hanging sign to closed.

"Shutting early?" Lane asked, looking up when he heard the lock click into place. It was barely three.

"Can't work too late on a holiday, now, can we?" Gayle announced with exaggerated drama before she began climbing the stairs up to their apartment.

Lane waited for her to elaborate—it was only October 3rd—but, when she failed to do so, he turned to Dawn instead.

"It's our fiftieth anniversary," Dawn explained. "Well, seventh, legally, you know how it is. But we had our own unofficial ceremony back in the seventies."

"Oh, congratulations!" Lane wished he had something better to give them than salutations. "That's seriously impressive."

"Impressive she's put up with me for this long." Gayle came back through the door at the top of the stairs, her arms full of premade party platters and a pitcher of punch. Before she could even ask, Lane jogged up the stairs and took most of the items from her.

"We were hoping you'd stay and celebrate with us?" Dawn asked as she cleared space on the counter for Lane to put his armfuls down.

He faltered, surprised. "Don't you want to do something more than just hang out here with me? Fifty is a big deal."

"Believe it or not, we quite like it here." Gayle set down the last of the platters.

Dawn was moving one of the t-shirt racks to the side, clearing a large square of floor space. "And we quite like you, too."

Lane ducked his head at the compliment. "Yeah but—"

"We won't be offended if you have more exciting plans."

He could tell Dawn meant the remark sincerely. She hadn't meant to remind him that his only plans were to pile on three layers of sweatshirts and play mindless puzzle games on his phone in the back of his car all night.

"I think I can clear some time."

Gayle clapped Lane on the back with a grin. He was getting used to how much that stung, not bothering to hide his wince before smiling back and helping her pull the plastic wrap and container lids off the food. There was well enough for the whole town, let alone three people.

From the back of the shop, the dark and eerie folk record cut short mid-lament. It had been an album called

You Are Free, though Lane had yet to figure out if "Cat Power" was the name of the lead singer or the band—he had added it to the growing list of groups he had never heard of but came to love through the shop. After a brief moment of debate, Dawn replaced the record with another, and the light rhythmic bell tones of a vibraphone filled the silence.

Slowly, the warm swell of a cello joined. The sound filled every corner of the shop rising and falling with only the slightest of trills. Lane could feel the vibrations of it in his chest as the cello fell away, replaced by what he believed was an oboe.

"We got married to this song," Dawn remarked, spinning slowly in a circle as she made her way back to the front counter.

"The first time," Gayle added with a wink as she took Dawn's outstretched hand and spun her, following her out back to the cleared space of the makeshift dance floor.

"Kay Gardner." Dawn spun once more as the cello and oboe began to play in rounds with each other. "An icon."

Lane made another note on his phone.

Pulling a stool around to the side of the counter, he sat perched, absentmindedly snacking on baby carrots while he watched the couple dance.

They were beautiful.

That was his first thought. He had never given much

thought to growing old—never believed he would, if he were being honest—but if there had ever been a couple who aged gracefully, he was sure it was them. Not that they were necessarily spry for their age. Gayle had a decided limp—a bad hip replacement she complained about periodically—and Dawn had to pause mid-song to catch her breath and rest. But when they danced, they moved in perfect sync. Gayle's hand rested comfortably on the small of Dawn's back, Dawn's head was tilted down slightly, the exact angle for her to look into Gayle's eyes. They laughed as they danced, not at jokes or witty comments but with the sheer joy of it. The music rose and fell, contemplative, confident, and comforting.

Lane couldn't help but smile.

He tapped his fingertips against a cup of punch in time with the bell tones of the vibraphone, content to simply sit and appreciate the moment, but Gayle and Dawn had other plans. They made a slow rotation around the room, circling closer to the counter. Letting go of Dawn's waist, Gayle turned her so she could reach out and offer her hand to Lane.

"Care for a dance?"

He swallowed the bit of carrot he had been chewing and shook his head. "I can't dance."

"You think I can?" Gayle snorted from Dawn's other

side.

Dawn rolled her eyes but didn't disagree. "That doesn't mean we don't try."

Before he could refuse, she grabbed his wrist and pulled him from his seat. He barely had a chance to set his glass of punch on the edge of a nearby display before Gayle caught his other hand and they began to dance.

The music shifted just as he joined them. The song that followed was light, upbeat, and spirited. Dawn, Gayle, and Lane turned in time with it as best they could. Laughing and clapping as the pair of women took turns spinning Lane back from one to the other. He let them, dizzy but smiling so wide his cheeks ached.

The song was building up to its climactic end, the three of them linking arms and shuffling side to side in some semblance of a dance line, when Lane took three steps back and knocked into the nearest display table. Laden, as it was, with records, the table only shuddered but it was enough to upend the mostly full glass of punch that had been sitting atop it. Lane flinched away in time, but the bright orange-red liquid spilled out onto Dawn's blouse and dripped down the front of the table onto the floor.

"Shit." Lane righted the cup and glanced around for any towels at hand. "Sorry! I'll clean it."

"No, no," Gayle put a hand on his arm, stopping him in

his tracks as he turned towards the basement door. "I'll get it."

"I really don't mind." Lane could tell she was out of breath from dancing. It didn't make sense that they'd invite him to celebrate their anniversary but wouldn't trust him to grab a mop.

"Don't you worry about it." Gayle shooed him away, grabbing the key from the counter and disappearing through the door. He couldn't help but frown after her.

"Hand me one of those shirts, won't you?" Dawn nodded towards the merchandise racks. She started to unbutton her blouse and Lane quickly turned away. He kept his eyes down as he held the shirt out to her. She took it with a slight chuckle. "I didn't spend my best years in the 60s just to be modest now."

Lane glanced up, his face still slightly red. Dawn was standing with her back to him, laying her stained blouse out on the display table. The sight of her made him freeze.

Her long white hair curled lightly around her shoulders. The skin of her back was surprisingly smooth. She was pale, the yellowed peach of her skin was speckled only slightly with liver spots and freckles. Except for around the band of her light pink bra and rising up from her hips, she had very few wrinkles or stretch marks at all. The bareness was a contrast to the smattering of greyscale tattoos that hugged her shoulders and upper right arm; Lane had never seen her without long sleeves and would have been shocked by her tattoos—had it not been for the scars.

Four massive ridges raked across her back, banishing any thought he may have given to her wrinkles or tattoos. The jagged pink scars stood raised, slicing from the base of her neck and disappearing under the high-waisted band of her skirt. Lane didn't understand how someone could be so badly injured and survive.

Dawn slipped the store shirt over her head, the scars vanishing beneath it. Lane averted his eyes as she turned back around but the melancholy smile she gave him proved his look hadn't gone unnoticed.

"We spent our honeymoon, our first one, backpacking across Turkey," Dawn explained. She folded her stained blouse in her arms and shivered. "We had pitched a tent on the Anatolia Plateau, near the Library of Celsus. Trespassing, technically."

She put a finger to her lips and winked. Lane chuckled in spite of himself, his initial shock at the sight of her scars fading.

"Did you know wolves are almost extinct in Western Turkey?" The door to the basement opened and Gayle reappeared with a mop and paper towels. Dawn looked over his shoulder as Lane went to take the towels out of Gayle's hands. "I was just telling Lane about Turkey and how incredibly unlucky we were."

"Unlucky?" Gayle frowned, leaning on the mop to catch her breath. "We were pretty damn lucky that group of archeologists had a medic with them."

"True enough." Dawn helped wipe down the top of the table while Lane crouched and cleaned off the front of the glass display. He looked up as she continued, "Gayle had gone to see the ruins when the wolf found our camp. There was a research team there she brought for help."

Gayle shuddered. "I'll never forget the sound."

"Sound?" Lane straightened, paling, as he took the mop from her. He could only imagine what she meant. Howling. Snarls. The screaming.

"I think that's enough reminiscing for one evening." Dawn cleared her throat and tossed her handful of paper towels into a nearby waste bin. "We're all together and in good health. I think that's enough reason to celebrate, don't you?"

"Of course." Gayle took Dawn's hand in hers. The look they shared made Lane avert his gaze.

He leaned the mop against the table and left them to their moment, moving to replace another of the display racks Dawn had moved to clear space for a dance floor.

"You can leave that," Dawn called out at the sound of the rubber display legs squeaking across the hardwoods. "We can put it back in the morning."

"I don't mind," Lane protested even as he returned to the front of the store. The couple was boxing up the mountain of food that remained.

"You can't do it now." Gayle dropped the containers into his arms. "Your hands are full."

"But—"

"They'll go to waste here," Dawn insisted, adding a bag of chips to the top of his burden.

Lane tried to graciously refuse again but, after a chorus of shushing from both women, he relented. "Thank you."

Together, Dawn and Gayle saw him to the door, thanking him for the dance and offering—without success—to give him paper and plasticware to go with the food. He didn't have the heart to tell them that most of the dips and cut fruit would spoil in a few days.

"Happy anniversary!" Lane waved with his elbow as they held the door for him to back through to the sidewalk. He packed the food into the backseat of his car and glanced towards the shop as he slammed the door shut.

The day had darkened to dusk and the warm glow of the shop lights cast amorphous shadows through the Halloween-themed window stickers and signs. Through the gaps, he could see Gayle and Dawn still dancing. They held each other close, Gayle's head upon Dawn's shoulder, swaying to the sound of music that trickled out slow and soft onto the street.

Lane was still smiling when he pulled into the empty field and laid down to sleep in the backseat of his car. The cold light of the waxing moon diffused out through the clouds as he wrapped himself in old blankets and sweatshirts, falling asleep warm below.

Track 6

Over the next week, the temperature in Slatington plummeted. Warm days and crisp Autumn evenings gave way to biting winds and frost-stiff mornings. Lane took to taking naps in the sauna at the YMCA or leaned up against the wall on a bench at the laundromat over sleeping in his car. He couldn't afford the gas to keep it running all night.

He wasn't above asking Dawn and Gayle for help—he would have gladly slept on a chair in the shop if they didn't want him crashing on their couch—but something had changed between them, as well.

Ever since they had celebrated the couple's anniversary together, both women had seemed distant. More than once, Lane had shown up for work to find one or both of them still in bed, either a note left for him on the counter to open or pinned to the outside of their apartment door. It was eerie, the first time he walked into the empty shop, but what was more distressing was how they treated him when they were around.

Cordial was how he was inclined to describe it. At least, that's how they had been at first. Gayle seemed reserved, her jibes turning curt when he least expected it, and Dawn no longer humored Lane with a laugh when he made obscure foreign film jokes. But they were still friendly. Lane had begun to wonder if they were just overworked or, he thought back to the menacing scars across Dawn's back, perhaps the week following their anniversary was always a somewhat somber time.

It wasn't until Gayle started to snap at him that Lane started to worry it was something else entirely.

Lane had been keeping his distance, as much as he could in the small shop, even going so far as to graciously refuse Dawn's offers for lunch; yet it still wasn't enough for him to avoid the reprimands they threw his way when he took too long to ring up a customer or when he inaccurately organized the new arrivals.

He was on edge. Constantly worrying about what he had done to earn such a change in their demeanors. He was so preoccupied that he hardly noticed when the usual group of high school freshmen blundered in through the door and out of the cold, huddling in the back of the shop by the stairs where it was warmest.

Lane was busy folding the latest shipment of t-shirts when Gayle came down from the apartment, grumbling to herself about the ache in her hip. The high schoolers were joking and shoving each other playfully around the shelves—not an unusual sight, though Lane typically tried to keep them in check when they got too rough. Gayle was stepping off of the last few steps when one of the high schoolers shoved another into the banister, which shook and knocked her off balance. In a slew of curses, she stumbled into the nearest table, managing to stay upright but duly bruising her arm in the process.

"Oh shit." The high schooler that was pushed into the banister reached out to offer her a hand. "My bad."

"You okay, Mrs. G?" The other kids gathered around as Gayle righted herself, swatting the offered hand away. "We didn't mean it."

"Get off of me," Gayle snapped. "This isn't a place for you to be wrestling like dogs."

"I'm sure it was just an accident." Lane left his post at the counter, something in Gayle's tone compelling him to intervene. After looking her over to make sure she truly wasn't hurt, he stepped between Gayle and the gaggle of children. "Are you all right?"

"I'd be better with those little shits out of my shop," Gayle snarled.

He gaped at her. The kids behind him roused, disgruntled.

"They'll be more careful from now on," Lane leveled a warning glare over his shoulder, "won't you?"

The group nodded, a few more apologies and promises

were forthcoming.

"They should have been more careful in the first place." Gayle didn't relent.

"They will be." Lane tilted his head towards the door. The kids behind him took the hint, shuffling out with another chorus of apologies. "I'll make sure to watch them next time they come in."

"You should have watched them this time." Gayle shoved away from the table. Lane flinched when the table, laden with boxes of records and miniature musician figurines, screeched nearly four inches across the floor. He knew she was fit for a woman her age but even he had trouble moving the display tables on his own.

He took a step back, recovering himself. "I'm sorry, I—"

"What would you have done if they had broken something?" She matched him step for step. Her demeanor so unexpected, so out of character, Lane couldn't stop a slight chill of fear from running down his spine. "What if I had broken something?"

"I'm sorry," he started again, grateful when the bell to the shop door chimed and Dawn returned from mailing their utility payments.

Lane shot an anxious look towards her over Gayle's shoulder. She met his eyes, grimaced, and rushed over to her wife's side.

Dawn took Gayle's arm—more to restrain than support her. "Why don't we go upstairs?"

"There were some kids messing around," Lane explained hurriedly as Dawn tried—and failed—to lead Gayle back towards the stairs. "I don't think they broke anything, but I should've been watching, I know, I—"

"It's fine," Dawn interrupted sharply. She seemed more concerned about wrangling Gayle than with Lane's explanation. "We'll talk about it later."

She finally managed to unstick Gayle from the spot. Lane could've sworn he heard the shorter woman actually growl. With some difficulty, Dawn helped her up the stairs. "Let's go."

Lane stood frozen until the couple disappeared behind their apartment door. He had never met anyone with dementia or any sort of degenerative cognitive illness. The last person he had expected to show symptoms of something like that was Gayle. Witty sassy Gayle. But he feared that was the only way to explain her sudden change of demeanor. That was the fear he had felt, he told himself, fear for her. Not of her. Taking a shaky breath, he lowered himself onto the bottom step. He could never be afraid of her.

But what if she was sick? Should he expect more

outbursts like that? Did Dawn know? Would she be okay? Would either of them?

Lane bounced his foot against the back of the step, tapping tapping tapping nervously as he waited for Dawn to come back down. The creak of the door above alerted him that she had.

"Is she okay?" He stood; one foot poised to ascend the other trailing on the floor.

Dawn nodded. She looked exhausted. "It's the weather. The cold exasperates her arthritis."

Lane just stared at her. That hardly explained Gayle's anger and certainly didn't explain the sudden burst of strength.

"Being in that amount of pain would make anyone a bit irritable," Dawn continued as if she could read the confusion on his face.

He moved out of the way as she descended the stairs. Something about her explanation didn't make sense. "Are you sure? I mean, she's been acting a little…"

"I'm sure." Dawn slid the display table back into place with a small grunt of effort. Lane began to wonder if he should start working out when he went to the gym. "I know how things may look, but please, don't take it personally."

"No, it's fine," Lane assured her, understanding the wave she directed at the door and flipping the sign to closed.

"I'm just worried about her."

"I appreciate that." Dawn leaned heavily on the counter. Her expression was so filled with open sincerity that Lane dropped his gaze to the floor. "Truly. But I'm sure in a week or so she'll be back to her old self, don't you worry."

Lane smiled and nodded along with her. He wanted to believe her optimism, to share it, but he couldn't help but feel that she was ignoring the symptoms of some much larger issue.

Still, he didn't have the heart to press her on it.

"How about you head home early," Dawn pulled back from the counter and started the process of closing out the register, "and I'll see if I can convince my wife to take a vacation."

"I'll see you tomorrow?"

Dawn shrugged. "I've nowhere else to be."

Track 7

Lane arrived at the shop the next day to find the door locked and an envelope taped to its glass. Inside, he found a key and a note.

"Lane, we're sorry for the inconvenience, but can you mind the shop for the rest of the week? We will be upstairs in case of emergencies. I'm sure you're capable enough to handle it, though. Things will be back to normal in a few days."

He recognized Dawn's small, slanted handwriting. Bouncing the small key on his palm, he frowned and mulled over her final assurance.

"Things will be back to normal in a few days."

No matter how strongly he wanted to believe that, the stark decline of their attitudes over the past week had him entirely unconvinced.

The key fit snugly into the lock, letting out an audible click as he opened the shop door. Lane went through the usual routine, filling the cash register with change from the safe, picking a record—Marika Hackman's *We Slept at Last* was one of his favorites from their pile of seasonal spooky options—to play throughout the morning, and turning on all the decorative lights and signage hanging in the windows. It felt strange going through the motions alone.

True, he had opened the shop alone before, but most of the time they had unlocked the store that morning. To leave him a key meant that they didn't expect to leave their apartment for at least a day or two. That, in and of itself, was unusual.

Yet, throughout the course of the day, Lane heard noises that struck him as even stranger. In the quiet minutes when one record ended and the music gave way to the scratch ticking of the needle, Lane could hear muffled banging and what sounded like arguments coming from the rooms above the shop. Never any words. He never made out a particular phrase or shout from the apartment, but he was so certain that he heard Gayle and Dawn fighting that, more than once, he climbed the stairs to the apartment and raised his fist to knock.

He never did.

Each time the sounds quieted down by the time he reached the top of the stairs and, remembering Dawn's note and her remark about emergencies, he returned to the ground floor and started another record.

As the day progressed, the sky beyond the window darkened well beyond the overcast of a typical October day. The rain came first. It fell so heavily that Lane could hardly make out the shapes of cars passing along Main Street through the torrent and diffused light of the street and headlights. The wind followed, whistling through the alleys between the shop and its adjoining businesses. Thunder and lightning solidified the abrupt Autumn storm. Lane sat on the stool frowning at the glowing "open" sign in the window. A flood warning would be more likely to come than a customer.

Lane's dismal mood grew with every minute of pouring rain. If the ground was wet, he wouldn't be able to move his car into the field. There were few parking lots not monitored by towing companies that were also dark enough to allow sleep. He considered staying the night in the shop—especially since Gayle and Dawn didn't plan on coming down any time that evening—but he couldn't overcome his conscience. Until he asked for their permission, it would be a breach of trust; he didn't have the wherewithal to intrude upon them to ask.

But the storm was growing worse. The trees that spotted the road outside whipped back and forth, a bang from the back of the shop made Lane jump, and trash was swept up through the alley as it rolled out of the fallen can. Lane was switching the record over to what would likely be the last album of the night when a loud crash shattered the muted beating of the rain.

A gust of wind swept through the shop, the sound of the

storm crescendoing sharply. Lane spun around, dropping the record back into place. Glass scattered across the floor. Rain blew in through the shattered side window, a large tree branch lay at odd angles in the middle of the shop floor.

"Shit." Lane ran over to the window and pulled all of the moveable shelves and tables he could away from the incoming rain. The legs scraped against the floor, and he hoped belatedly that they wouldn't leave scratches.

He tore through the closets and found a plastic tablecloth covered in miniatures of the Full Moon Records logo. Secured with packing tape, it was enough to keep out the rain until the storm passed. However, there was nothing to sweep up the glass or to dry the water that had already pooled along the wall.

All of the cleaning supplies were in the basement.

Lane stared at the unassuming door from the bottom of the steps up to Dawn and Gayle's apartment. Dawn had told him not to bother them unless it was an emergency. Did the window count? They couldn't do anything until the storm ended, anyway, and it certainly wasn't an emergency to use a broom and a towel. After all of the banging and arguing he had heard throughout the day, Lane would much rather face a not-up-to-code basement than interrupt his bosses' solitude.

They kept the key in a drawer in the front counter. It

didn't take him long to find, tucked under the empty stack of deposit bags, as it was. Lane ran his thumb over the teeth of the key as he made his way to the basement door. He paused for only a moment, trying to shake off the nerves that came from knowingly disobeying the only true rule Dawn and Gayle had ever set for him.

The key turned in the lock with a satisfying clunk.

The door was heavier than Lane had expected; he leaned back, using his body weight to force it, creaking, open. Inside, the stairs descended into darkness. He stepped down onto the top stair to turn on the light, resting his hand against the interior of the door, and stopped. There was soft egg-crate foam lining the backside of the door, the kind used to soundproof recording rooms and soundstages. Lane ran his fingers across the plush surface, frowning. With his other hand, he reached in through the doorway and found the light switch.

Bright fluorescent tube lights lined the walls of the stairwell. Lane blinked at the glow, stark against the dim atmosphere of the shop that had nothing more than a few low-level Halloween lights and the streetlamps to illuminate it. The stairwell looked pristine. A single steel railing trailed the left-hand wall and the stairs themselves were carpeted with thick white shag. As Lane began to descend, he held onto the railing, his knuckles brushing the wall. It was an odd sensation. He reached out and pressed his fingertips into what he had thought was simple white-painted drywall. He was wrong. The wall itself had give, dimpling under his hand like taut pillowed suede. Each step down to the sealed cement landing made him both more confused and ill at ease.

Lane stepped down onto the cement. His footsteps sounded staccato, the strange noise-dampening walls and carpet of the stairs catching and muffling all reverberations. As he rounded the corner to face what he expected to be a cluttered and neglected basement, reality stopped him in his tracks.

There was a single room, massive, sterile, with glistening cement on the floor, ceilings, and walls. Between him and the room were metal bars, shining like silver, that spanned from floor to ceiling with only a small gap, a single missing bar, to allow anyone to pass through. The bars on either side of the gap were tarnished to a spotty brown. Lane slipped through the gap, his heart pounding in his ears as he passed the small shelf of cleaning supplies by his elbow and stared in horror at two massive metal structures positioned side by side in the center of the room.

Cages.

Two identical metal cages, black iron nearly as tall as the room, sat imposing, like something from the first season of *Hemlock Grove*. Inside were piles of rusted chains and shackles large enough to encircle Lane's waist. One set per cage.

"What the fuck?" Lane let out a shaky breath, slowly moving towards the nearest cage.

Closer, he could see the floor inside the cage was not the sterile, shining, sealed concrete of the rest of the room. There was a large, grated drain in the center. Gashes as wide as Lane's arm broke the surrounding smooth surface, dark brown-black stains filling into the porous scars of the broken seal.

He circled the cages, each step a staccato tick tick tick in the stillness. His mind was numb as he tried to rationalize why Dawn and Gayle would have something so gruesome, so horrifying, in their basement. Recent outbursts aside, neither of them struck him as violent. Some sort of BDSM thing, then? Anything seemed more reasonable than...whatever the fuck cages of that size were made for. The bars were so thick, Lane couldn't even wrap his fingers all the way around them.

It was with difficulty that he tore his eyes away from the cages to the only other object in the room. A six-foot-long chest freezer sat along the far wall. Whatever Dawn and Gayle used the cages for, maybe he would find some sort of answer in there.

Placing one hand near either corner of the lid, Lane flexed his fingers against the white textured metal and hefted the top open. He shoved the lid back so it rested open against the wall, stumbling backward away from the sight. It was overflowing with meat.

Not meat. Animals.

Opossums, raccoons, squirrels, and the bottom half of a deer were piled in mounds on top of each other. Their skin was torn, bones broken, blood streaked across fur and freezer walls. Roadkill. The flecks of metal embedded in their skin and the litany of flattened bodies proved it.

Lane gagged at the sight, though the freezer dampened the smell.

"Fuck this."

Lane slammed the lid of the freezer back into place and practically ran for the door.

He slipped through the bars, forgetting the broom and dustbin he had come down for, and took the stairs two at a time. The door groaned shut as he threw his shoulder against it and clicked the lock back into place.

Lane slid to the floor, leaning against the door with his knees tucked close to his chest. There had to be something. Something random and obscure but totally reasonable and legal that he hadn't thought of to explain what he had seen in the basement. There had to.

The door at the top of the stairs rattled slightly in its frame. Lane jumped to his feet and sprinted across the shop, slamming the basement key back into its place in the drawer. He snatched the roll of packing tape off the counter and slid across the wet floor to the window.

"Hey," Lane called out, slightly out of breath, as Dawn appeared at the top of the stairs, "I was just about to get you. Storm blew a window out."

"I thought I heard something," Dawn responded. Lane had to strain to hear her over the wind.

For all his nerves and confusion about what he had found in the basement, the first thought that occurred to him when he saw Dawn slowly descending the stairs was that he was worried for her.

She was bundled up in a thick pink housecoat that looked like it would swallow up her thin and pallid frame. Her bright blue eyes were cloudy, heavy-lidded as she surveyed the damage from the covered window to the glass on the floor.

She reached the bottom of the staircase and instructed, almost as an afterthought, "Move away from there, please, I don't want you to cut yourself."

He did as she asked. Usually, he would have offered to clean it for her, but he was still reeling from what he had seen in the basement and was not at all inclined to go back down.

Still, he couldn't reconcile the appearance of the woman in front of him with the cages and piles of animal carcasses she and her wife were keeping down below.

"Are you all right?" Dawn's question broke through his thoughts. A flash of lightning illuminated her tired smile, transforming it into a grimace of glinting teeth. "You look like you've seen a ghost."

Lane nodded, turning his face away under the guise of checking the taped tablecloth for leaks. He had no idea what his expression might have conveyed. "Just startled me."

"Well, there's nothing we can do about it tonight." Dawn shivered and pulled her housecoat a little tighter around her. "Let's close for now and I'll call a repairman in the morning."

Lane mumbled something in acknowledgment. He wandered over to turn the sign on the door to "Closed" and to turn off their decorative and usual signage. The shop was cast in darkness, odd angles growing sharp and menacing with every flash of lightning.

"Gayle and I are going away for a few days." Dawn's hand on Lane's shoulder made him flinch. He covered his discomfort with a cough as he turned to face her. She continued, her gaze drifting off to the stormy sky behind him, "We booked some time at an overnight spa. I'll make sure to pay you your normal hours, I know this is sudden, but we'd rather keep the shop closed while we're gone."

"All right." Lane closed out the register, Dawn's hand still on his shoulder. He didn't remember her nails being so long or sharp. He was silently grateful for the time off. It would give him the chance to process what he had seen. Decide whether it was worth coming back.

"If the repairman comes while we're away, I might ask you to come in," Dawn added, her hand slipping from his arm. "If it's no trouble?"

"None at all." Lane shook his head and flashed her a quick forced smile. "I hope your trip is relaxing."

"Thanks." Dawn returned his smile with another glint of teeth. "Now head on out before the road gets any worse."

Lane didn't need any further coaxing. He said a quick farewell to Dawn before sprinting through the rain to his car. Falling, drenched, into the seat, he reached into his pocket and felt the hard steel of the shop key, cold, against his fingers. The teeth of the key dug painfully into the palm of his hands as he clenched his fists to keep his hands from shaking.

Track 8

Lane spent the rest of the night lying awake in the driver's seat of his car. He had parked in the very back of the YMCA parking lot, under a streetlight. After an hour of trying to sleep in the fully reclined seat, he gave up and took to searching police records. Missing people, missing pets, violent crimes, anything. The more he found the more idiotic he felt.

Slatington had a lower crime rate than most of the state, not counting burglary and petty theft. He certainly doubted that his elderly employers were nimble enough to be cat burglars. Nothing he found could be reasonably linked to cages and chains and a freezer of dead animals. If they were all part of some sort of kink, then that was one he had never heard of—and Lane thought himself fairly well-versed. He wasn't about to do an internet search for that, though.

The storm continued long into the night, whipping leaves and rain loudly against the car windows. At around a quarter after two in the morning, the power in that part of town went out. A tree across the line or a transformer struck by lightning. Lane and his car were plunged into total darkness. He waited until the last few figures fled and closed the YMCA, before sticking his keys in the ignition and starting the car.

It was a waste of gas he couldn't afford, but the darkness put him on edge. With every shadow flickering in the headlights, every snap of a branch falling against the pavement, he jerked forward in his seat. He should have called the police. In the basement, at the first sight of the oversized cages and rusted iron chains, he should have called someone. Anyone to help figure out what was going on.

Even as he repositioned his seat upright, his foot on the brake, his hand on the gearshift, Lane knew that he should do something to uncover what was going on in that basement.

But if Full Moon Records closed, if Dawn and Gayle fired him for intruding, if they were investigated, if they were arrested, then what else would he have?

Track 9

Two days after the storm had passed, Lane got a call from Dawn asking him to let in a repairman to fix the window that afternoon. She sounded even worse over the phone than she had the last time he saw her. Her voice was rough, and she spoke in short clipped sentences. Lane agreed then immediately regretted it. He still didn't know what to do about the cages in the basement. He had hoped to stay away longer to decide. To see if anything else came up, anything damning or vindicating. But he had no excuse to say no.

So, Lane found himself leaning against his car outside of Full Moon Records until the general contractor arrived.

"It's right in here." Lane waved the man who jumped from the lifted mud-covered pick-up truck over to the shop door. The man talked him through the basic expenses of what a replacement would entail—all of which Lane typed into his phone to tell Dawn and Gayle later—as he unlocked the shop door and led the contractor over to the covered window.

The glass was cleared from the floor, but the makeshift tarp remained. Lane glanced up at the apartment door, wondering if Dawn and Gayle were still away on their trip.

There were no sounds drifting down from above, no voices, no footsteps. Anything he may have heard was lost, however, as the contractor began extracting the frame of the shattered window. As the man worked, Lane sat behind the counter and stared at the basement door.

The paintings, the old metal doorknob, the sign—externally nothing had changed. Nothing to belie the strange and unnerving things kept within. Lane tapped his nails on the counter, a quick erratic rhythm.

When the contractor left to retrieve the replacement window—Dawn had apparently measured the opening for him ahead of time—Lane took the opportunity to dig through the counter drawer for the basement key. He wanted to double-check what he had seen. Maybe he had overreacted. Maybe he had missed something to explain away all the confusion and suspicion he harbored.

But the key wasn't there.

Glancing back over his shoulder to make sure the contractor was still at his truck, Lane walked over to the door. It was locked.

He tried again, jiggling the doorknob, remembering how difficult the door itself had been to move. It didn't budge.

The bell over the shop entrance rang. Lane jumped, spinning on his heel to face the rather bemused-looking contractor.

"Didn't mean to startle you," the man apologized, returning once more to the emptiness where the window had been.

"I was just going to get something for the dust," Lane felt the inexplicable need to make up an excuse, "but I think my bosses took the key with them."

"Nothing a screwdriver and a paperclip can't fix." The man laughed and Lane chuckled nervously along with him. Pausing mid-measurement, the contractor turned around and leveled a stern look at him. "Now I'm not telling you how to break into that lock. It was a joke, you hear me?"

"Yeah, of course." Lane held his hands up dismissively. "I know."

The contractor held his gaze for another second before shrugging and turning back to his work. "Have to say it. Liabilities and all that."

"Right, I get it."

Lane leaned back with his elbows against the counter, chewing on his bottom lip. He wouldn't be stupid enough to break into Dawn and Gayle's basement. He already regretted going down there in the first place. If they had locked the room and thrown away the key—or as was more likely, taken it with them—then more power to them. He was relieved. He wouldn't think of it again.

When the contractor finished, Lane helped him carry his tools out to the truck, making small talk and joking in that stiff and awkward way that two strangers joke. He waited until the man's truck had disappeared around the corner to re-lock the door to the shop.

As he turned away from the store, Lane dropped the shop key into his pocket where it clinked softly against the screwdriver he had stolen from the contractor's bag.

Track 10

When Lane returned that night to the shop, a perfectly circular moon shone so bright the streetlamps stayed sleeping, leaving Main Street striped with the deep blue shadows of buildings and telephone poles. He felt like a criminal, black hoodie layered over three flannels, stooped forward with his shoulder against the glass as he used his key to unlock the shop door.

He opened the door quickly, trying to slip in before anyone on the street saw, but the bell rang out in loud crystalline peals. It was blaring. Lane ducked down next to an oversized plastic pumpkin, waiting a full minute until his heart stopped pounding in his ears so he could be sure it wasn't footsteps running to stop him. Laughing nervously to himself, Lane rose to his feet and straightened the hem of his hoodie. He took a deep breath and circled around behind the counter. The drawer was still empty, the key nowhere to be found.

Lane pushed aside the pile of clear deposit envelopes and pulled out a paperclip, the weight of the filched screwdriver tugging down the front of his hoodie. As he walked to the back of the shop, he worked the paperclip straight and tried to recall all the tips and tricks he had learned from YouTube earlier that day. He tried the door again, hoping it would turn in his hand; if the door was left open, then nothing—no one—could be locked inside.

It didn't.

Not allowing the time to second-guess himself, Lane knelt by the door and set his phone screen-down on the ground, flashlight shining up to his face. Between the shadows, his inexperience, and sweaty palms, it took Lane at least ten minutes to make any sort of sense of what he was doing. Another five until he heard the lock click out of place.

He stretched as he stood. Gripping the handle with both hands, Lane used his body weight to force the door open.

The lights were already on. Lane paused on the top step. Even with the door open, the stairwell sounded different. There weren't voices, exactly, but the silence wasn't as perfect as it had been the day before. A subtle movement of air, the rustle of fabric, disruptions of stillness. Lane's stomach knotted, his worst fears flashing like some violent horror film behind his eyes.

He took the stairs slowly, ears pricked for every creak and potential clink of chain against cement. Lane took one last steadying breath and rounded the corner to face the silver gate. The freezer of animal carcasses. The empty cages.

They weren't empty.

Sitting, one in each cage, Dawn and Gayle huddled on the concrete floor, leaning against the bars closest to each other. They both were wrapped in heavy down blankets but, from the pale exposed skin of Dawn's back and the bare length of Gayle's legs, Lane could tell they were naked beneath. He could see the top of Dawn's scars rising up her back and another, single scar, following the curve of Gayle's inner thigh and disappearing beneath the blanket. Around their shoulders, wrists, and ankles, the iron shackles pinned them down. The largest sat so low on Dawn's shoulders it looked as though she could slip right through. Piles of animal carcasses along each cage wall opposing the women seeped blood into the breaks and gashes in the floor as they thawed.

Lane let out a sound somewhere between a gasp and a scream. Both women turned, two pairs of amber eyes staring back at him. Gayle struggled to her feet under the weight of the chains, the blanket hanging loosely from her shoulders.

"Lane?"

Her voice snapped him out of his shock. He rushed over to Gayle's cage, bruising his shoulder as he pushed through the gap in the silver gate, ignoring his confusion, fear, and horror.

"How did you get down here?" Dawn's voice was hoarse, panicked. She tried to stand but couldn't.

Lane scrambled to find a latch or a lock on the cage door. It was a simple bolt held in place by a notch in the casing. Gayle could have easily reached through the bars to open it. She did reach through the bar, grabbing Lane's wrist the moment his hand touched the metal.

"Get out." Her grip was so strong it hurt.

"Let me get you out of here." Lane ignored her, trying to open the lock even as she held him in place. He couldn't think of anything else except helping them. The explanations would have to come later.

"Listen to her, Lane," Dawn pleaded. She was clinging to the bars as if they would help her stand but the weight of the iron was too much. "You have to go, it's not safe."

"What's going on?" Lane gave up on the lock and caught Gayle's hand in his as he looked back and forth between her and her wife. His voice was shrill and terrified. "What the fuck is going on?"

"We'll explain everything, but not now." Dawn winced, a rough loud cough tearing through her body. It seemed to take all her strength to push herself across the floor to the far side of the cage. "You have to leave. Go upstairs, lock the door, and don't come down."

"But—"

"Please." Gayle pulled away from him, also retreating as far as the cage would allow. A tremor shook through her entire body, and she collapsed to the floor with a gasp of pain and clang of metal. When she stared up at him, the light seemed to reflect against the black of her pupils. Her voice was small. "We don't want to hurt you."

"That doesn't even make sense!" But he could feel his heart pounding in his chest, an icy numbness settling in his limbs. The hair on his arms stood on end. Every instinct was telling him to run.

"Please," Gayle repeated, another violent convulsion sending her gasping to the floor.

In the opposing cage, Dawn screamed.

Lane reached out for the lock on her door but Dawn lunged at him. She jumped to her feet, teeth bared—too long, too sharp—but the weight of the chains pulled her back down to the ground.

She snarled. "Get out. Now."

He backed away, each step slow and faltering. The two women writhed in pain, convulsions growing faster and stronger. Lane couldn't bring himself to leave. He slipped back behind the silver gate. A fear greater than anything he had ever felt pinned him behind the bars.

Lane sank to his knees. Trying to force the terror down,

to go and let them out, to call a doctor, anything, anything at all.

"Go!" Dawn shouted, breaking off in a gasp of pain. She spun away from him and the blanket fell from her shoulders. He could see the vertebrae of her spine stretching taut her wrinkled skin.

Lane didn't move. His voice broke. "I just want to help you."

From the cage closest, Gayle let out a whine like an animal in pain. Lane could see blood running down from her nail beds as she gripped the bars of the cage. Her nails curled long, like claws.

She met his eyes and managed to smile. "You can't."

Track 11

Lane knelt behind the silver gate for hours, made mute by horror and awe as he watched the two women's bodies tear themselves apart.

Bones snapped and bent and fused. Muscles rippled, stitching and unstitching into unnatural shapes. Skin tore open, slipping to the floor in mounds of steam and blood and fat. Dawn and Gayle bore the pain as long as they could before the screams began. At one point, early on, Lane climbed the stairs and shut the soundproof basement door. He could have left.

He didn't.

In the absence of flesh grew fur. Thick coarse fur with strands as long as his arm. It covered the women from head to toe in ripples of black, brown, grey, and silver. Flecked with drops of red and bits of yellowed fat. The screaming stopped, giving way to deep-throated snarls and blood-curdling howls.

The creatures writhed in the last pangs from the change. Lapping at the blood on their fur and on the floor, they devoured everything within the cages. From the animals to their very own skin. Once they had finished, they paced, growling and glaring each other down across the gap between the cages.

Lane stood, pressing his face against the silver bars of the gate, and the two animals—the two women—both snapped their attention toward him. He had to raise his chin to meet their glowing amber eyes. Two massive bipedal wolves, their hind legs too long, hunched over, panting with sharpened teeth and lolling tongues. Silver muzzles. Silky darkened fur. They were unlike anything Lane had ever seen.

They were beautiful.

Track 12

The change lasted until sometime before six in the morning, preceding the day's astronomical twilight. Lane watched, wide-eyed, as the wolves sank to the floor, shivering and whimpering as the fur shed from their bodies in clumps and soft washes.

Dawn and Gayle curled naked amidst the piles of fur and blood. Their skin was bruised and shining in a thin sheen of sweat. The oversized shackles, no longer digging into muscular wolfskin, held their limbs at odd angles as they tried to move, sliding and struggling on the slick cement floor. The wrinkles and loose skin of old age now seemed stretched, oversized for the fragile bones of their human bodies. One of them was crying softly. The sight was reminiscent of being born.

After some struggle, Gayle managed to push herself into a relatively upright position. She vomited a puddle of blood and fur onto the floor. Dawn was still curled on her side, her crying muffled into soft gasps and shivers.

Once the gagging had stilled, Gayle turned towards the other cage and tried to stand. The weight of the chains was too much. Her hands were too slick with gore to find traction on the cage bars.

Lane moved without thinking. His muscles stiff, his mind numb, he slipped between the bars of the silver gate and opened the door to Gayle's cage. She stared at him silently with wide brown eyes as he crossed through remnants of the carnage and knelt by her side. He could feel the blood soaking through the knees of his jeans as he unclasped the shackles from her body.

He draped the blanket over her shoulders and then lifted her into his arms. His shoes squeaked bloody footprints on the floor as he carried her over to the other cage. She leaned heavily on him as he set her on unsteady feet to unlock the second door. As soon as it was open, Gayle left Lane's side and stumbled as quickly as she could to kneel beside Dawn's shivering body.

She pulled Dawn close, cradling her head in her lap as she pulled the blanket from her shoulders and draped it over her wife. Gayle leaned over her, cooing soft loving comforts, as she smoothed her hair away from her face and wiped the blood and grime from her skin.

Lane followed, slowly, trying to be as unobtrusive as possible as he knelt by their sides and removed the shackles from around Dawn's limbs and neck. Gayle pointed him to a set of keys beside two folded robes on top of the chest freezer. He nodded, leaving the two women alone in each other's arms while he climbed the stairs and emerged into the warm light of early morning.

He blinked, staring out at the stillness of the shop and the normalcy of the cars passing by on the street. Belatedly, he looked over his shoulder and saw the bright red stains his shoes had left on the shag stairs. Lane left his shoes inside the basement door and continued on. He climbed the stairs to their apartment, unlocked the door, and made his way to the bathroom.

His arms full of towels, ibuprofen, and water bottles, Lane descended back into the basement. Voices drifted up, tired and worried, but by the time he was close enough to make out the words, they had stopped. He turned the corner to find Dawn and Gayle, bloody and robed, sitting side by side on top of the chest freezer. They stared at him warily, unmoving, as he squeezed through the gate, awkward with the bulk of his burden.

Lane crossed the distance, stopping several feet away from them, trying not to look at the cages or the gore within. His mind was blank. There were no words to describe what he had just witnessed, no way for him to comprehend it and all its implications, certainly not without time. The silence stretched on, and he could feel the two women watching him.

Glancing up at them, his eyes alighted on the smears of blood on their robes. He held the towels out towards them, though still too far away for them to reach. Lane was surprised when his voice didn't shake.

"I thought you'd want towels."

Dawn and Gayle exchanged a bewildered look. Dawn stood, her hand steadying her on Gayle's shoulder, and reached out for one of the towels. Each movement was slow and deliberate, as if she was worried she would scare him away.

She inclined her head, her eyes glistening. "Thank you."

Lane tried to smile but he wasn't exactly sure what expression he achieved.

Gayle followed, less deliberate than her wife, and took the second towel with a disgruntled huff. "I was hoping for a toothbrush."

Track 13

"It was during our honeymoon. The wolf wasn't a normal wolf, not that we knew that at the time. A month later, out of nowhere, I—"

Dawn broke off, leaning over to kiss Gayle on the cheek, her brow furrowed with guilt. Lane was sitting with the pair of them at their small round kitchen table, a pot of tea rested in the space between them. After the couple had regained a bit more of their strength, he had helped them out of the basement and waited while they showered and changed into clean clothes. The two women had kept a watchful eye over him, as if expecting him to run or scream or react in any expected way. But he simply sat, listened, and helped to pull the teacups down from the top shelf.

"Now we're in it together." Gayle squeezed Dawn's hand and kissed her, smiling extra wide to prove that all had been forgiven.

"Still, it took us a while to come to terms with it." Dawn turned her attention back to Lane. "I know it's difficult to believe. Which is why I'm surprised you seem to be handling it...okay."

"Are you?" Gayle prompted when Lane failed to comment.

"Okay?" He looked up from his reflection in his tea. They nodded. He let out a single laugh and shook his head. Nothing about what had happened in that basement was "okay."

"We understand it's frightening," Gayle began, an edge in her voice, "but we don't hurt people. There's no reason to get anyone else involved."

"You never have to see us again," Dawn added hurriedly. "We'll leave town, if that's what you want. We never wanted you to see that, we never meant for you to get involved—"

Lane stood, the scuffing of the chair cutting off Dawn's apology. He paced back and forth across the tight-packed kitchen. That wasn't what he wanted. Yes, he was scared— he was fucking terrified—but it wasn't entirely for the reasons they seemed to think.

"I've been living in my car."

He returned to the table and sat cross-legged in his chair. The confusion was plain on their faces. Lane looked down, picking at the frayed hem of his jeans. The words came out in a single bitter breath:

"For months. I've been living off of leftovers and vending machine shit. Scouring parking lots for change for laundry. I've been 'sneaking into' the men's locker room at the gym to shower with a membership under my deadname that expires in December. And I don't know if there's anyone else in this fucking town who would give a shit if I up and vanished. Who would even notice! And I—"

He gritted his teeth and forced himself to meet their eyes.

"And I don't know if I would be here if it weren't for you and this place." He gestured towards the door that led out to the shop. "And I'm not okay because if you leave, then...then there really wouldn't be anyone left."

Dawn reached out slowly, as if she were still afraid that putting her hand on his arm too quickly would frighten him, but Gayle was out of her seat as fast as she could. She pulled Lane into her arms, hugging him tight against her chest.

"I'm so sorry," Dawn murmured over and over again, rubbing her thumb in circles on his skin. He wanted to tell her that they had nothing to apologize for, but there was a lump in his throat too thick to speak past.

"Why on earth were you sleeping in your car?" Gayle's voice was shaking despite the forced snark in her tone.

"There's a Murphy bed in the spare room." Dawn circled the table and wrapped her arms around the both of them, Lane tucked in the center of their embrace.

"I didn't know that." Lane laughed in spite of himself, the tears he had been holding back finally spilling over.

All of the nerves and fear and confusion and—stronger

and stranger than them all—the relief crashed down on him. He broke down sobbing, crying harder every time Dawn and Gayle patted his back or ran their hands through his hair. Several minutes passed before he had composed himself to talk again.

He tried to mimic Gayle's earlier levity, but he was still hiccupping from crying, "Why on— earth do you keep— all the cleaning supplies in the— basement if you don't— want anyone to go down there?"

Gayle snorted as if the topic had come up many times before, but Dawn simply wiped her eyes and looked down at him indignantly. "Things are best kept where they're needed most."

Lane laughed, his lungs aching as the hiccups persisted. With a final squeeze of his shoulder and a light kiss on the top of his head, Dawn and Gayle returned to their seats across the table. Their expressions were serious once more, though not quite as severe as before, and Lane tried to brace himself. He wasn't sure his frayed nerves could handle much else.

"Speaking of," Gayle began, clearing her throat to hide the tinge of embarrassment in her voice, "I wanted to thank you. For earlier."

"The change is...difficult," Dawn continued, shuddering slightly at the memory of it, "but recently, well, old age is never easy. It would be a great help, to us, to have someone around."

"We never planned on asking you, or anyone, but," Gayle interrupted with a shrug, "I guess the wolf's out of the bag."

The implied offer startled and moved him, but his answer came almost without thinking. "As long as you stop making *Twilight* references."

Gayle chuckled. "Ah, but you do get them."

Lane's grin was fleeting, leveling out so that they would know he wasn't taking their request lightly. He reached out across the table and took Dawn and Gayle's hands in his. There was no question. No doubt, no matter how impossible it all should have been. He knew what he saw, and he understood how much he had to lose.

And what was one night a month compared to the prospect of home?

The End

About the Author

Sarah Edmonds is a queer author and filmmaker from southeastern Pennsylvania who currently serves as video poetry editor for the *West Trade Review* and as Editor-in-Chief of *For Page & Screen Magazine*. Her films have been featured in several international festivals and her writing has been published by, or is forthcoming with, Wolfsinger Publication's *Us/Them Anthology*, *Ethel Zine*, *West Trade Review*, *Decoded: Pride Anthology*, and Black Spot Books' *Under Her Eye* poetry showcase, among others.

About the Publisher

Thirty West Publishing House

Handmade Chapbooks (and more) since 2015

www.thirtywestph.com / thirtywestph@gmail.com

Review our books on Amazon & Goodreads

@thirtywestph

Fall of Fiction 2023

Bardo by Joseph Edwin Haeger
(ISBN-13: 979-8-9861105-7-8)

Late Nights at Full Moon Records by Sarah Edmonds
(ISBN-13: 979-8-9861105-9-2)

Lizard People by Ryan Rivas
(ISBN-13: 979-8-9861105-8-5)

~

Fall of Fiction 2022

Broke Witch by Jessica Bonder
(ISBN-13: 979-8-9861105-3-0)

How to Keep Time by Kevin M. Kearney
(ISBN-13: 979-8-9861105-1-6)

Tentacles Numbing by Shome Dasgupta
(ISBN-13: 979-8-9861105-2-3)

Printed in the USA
CPSIA information can be obtained
at www.ICGtesting.com
LVHW091730150724
785579LV00004B/86